VINTAGE OF MY YEARS

RON UNRUH

RON UNRUH

Cover oil painting by Ron Unruh.
Entitled, "Church in the Heart of the Vineyards" -St. Jacques Le Majeur,
Hunawihr, Alsace France.

Continuous Line drawings obtained royalty-free.

DEDICATION

Thank you for your encouragement, Christine.
You cheer me on.

PREFACE

The poems in this collection are whimsical, amusing, romantic and sometimes solemn. I have written them while living life, so they are distinctively mine. Yet many poems contain themes with which you will identify. They are honest and uncomplicated.

Vintage is a suitable term for this compilation. Whereas a wine maker uses the term 'vintage' to specify the year in which grapes are harvested and turned into an appealing wine, I use the word 'vintage' to define from my long life, a variety of sensations I have experienced. I will turn 82 in 2024. Like a wine, life within the poems is refined, graceful, and well-balanced. In my words, you will notice a trace of timelessness, a hint of quality, a note of character.

I fashioned the book to contain four movements of life: Life As it Is, Life As I Like it, Life As It Was, and Life As It Will be.

I hope you smile, wipe a tear, and then smile again.

Ron Unruh

FORWARD

In a literary and artistic sense, the poet is a romantic. When he retired in 2008, Ron's long-abandoned brushes, palette and empty canvasses solicited his attention. Pacific coastal landscapes and agricultural panoramas are featured in Ron's art and poetry. As Christine and Ron have travelled, scenes of people and places have translated into oil on canvas and story lines on paper. Five grandchildren living nearby feed Ron's heart with ideas and pleasure.

Words were Ron's preoccupation for fifty years as a pastor and teacher. He wrote poetry as a youth. In this, Ron's first published poetry collection, themes from 81 years of life are gathered in four sections: Life As It Is, Life As I Like It, Life As It Was, and, Life As It Will Be. A Back Story accompanies some poems to provide a context for the ideas expressed within.

I am sure that you will appreciate the sentiments emoted in this compilation.

Raison Detre
Editor in Chief, Unruh Publishing

CONTENTS

Dedication
Foreword

1
LIFE
AS IT IS

HIGH CLOUDS

High clouds, wisps, and Sun,
  a welcome warm September breeze.
    Retired now and free to enjoy
      autumn pleasures once withheld.
So many tasks, work to be done,
  Significant causes I thought then.
    Different days now, not salaried,
      pleased that sunshine today is free.

SUMMER'S DAY

As summer days go this one is good
with sunshine tonic for my mood,
and Pacific air to revive my drive,
I am delighted to be alive.
Tranquil morning invites my time,
sometimes prose and sometimes rhyme,
composing words as spa tunes play
faintly, wordlessly through summer's day.

LONG AGO US AND NOWADAY WE

Supremely moved by the beauty of this woman
In a long-ago time, by a long ago me.
She walked and spoke and sang,
Unaffected by me, independent and free,
Captivatingly true to herself.

No intention to charm, she enchanted me,
To the point of fixation, every waking moment.
She was in my mind and thoughts and dreams,
Yet I was not essential or desirable to her.
She had aspiring dreams of her own.

Admired by others, but I on the margin,
I cannot recall my youthful heroic,
That ventured that fearful approach,
That she interpreted as deserving enough
For a few hours from her life.

Her hours converted to our days of young love,
That birthed a shared hope of a life,
Based on promises, mine to her and hers to me,
And this unadorned future unfolded with pleasure,
Yet with the flexing and challenges normal to life.

All these years later we have each other,
Cherishing a long ago romance with joy.
Then decades of memories of family and achievements
And conjoint gratitude for love and patience,
That empowered us to never give up.

IT JUST HAPPENED

As Christine and I were saying goodnight
She with her head resting on her pillow,
And me reclining on mine,
With one hand she stroked the side of my face,
"Silly little beard," she said.

As she moved her hand against me
Her eyes held a hint of pathos,
Viewing the different me that she saw,
From the young new lover she recalled.
Her expression so clear to me that I said,
"I'm sorry."

Looking into her eyes, still stunningly dark and alluring
I said, "I tried not to change."
Her understanding eyes began to tear up
As she replied, "Me too."
"I know" I offered, "we tried for so long
not to let it happen to us."

And here we were, both happy with one another.
Both complete with memories made together.
Both nostalgic and yet realistic.
I said, "We'll go the rest of the way together."
At which time, we both wiped some tears.
And then Christine said, "Oh stop it,
You can talk like that when we are eighty."

Back Story: We are now 80 and 81. This poem was written 2010.

MORNING COFFEE & CHRISTINE

What would I do without her?
How could I live?
Yet people do go on I know,
        after a loved one is gone.
She sits outside my window
        sipping coffee in the morning, pensive.
           Her profile so familiar to me.

I envision that image missing and stop.
           I can't bear the thought and won't.
Even now my desktop bears her portrait,
    happy, smiling in the sunshine by the water.

That's my girl, the young yesterday girl,
same person, seasoned, wiser and so lovely.
           I loved her then and love her now, more deeply,
                With the memories of our years.

OUR HUMMINGBIRDS

With mild winters they avoid migration.
Feeding and fluttering they entertain
year round at our red feeding station,
since seasonally, the forecast is for rain.
Though today began with heavy snow,
predictably, they were here again.
These impressive petite creatures know,
to protect themselves from all conditions,
perching sheltered from the winter blow.
Under our warm eaves they find positions,
until they're airborne to fight a foe.
Other hummingbirds have ambitions.
Our neighbours put out feeders, so,
while ownership of hummingbirds makes no sense,
they're our birds, we say in smug defense.

ONE RECENT ORDINARY DAY

No one here but us at Mud Bay today.
With tide water out, at water's edge
scavenging birds leave opened shells
to dry under cloudless sky with snow tipped peaks
in the distance; a train's approach and ducks lift silently
and turn away.

From White Rock comes the Amtrak,
horn echoing in the hills through Crescent Beach,
across the bridge, around the bay, passengers' faces
savouring delights of sparkling waters and sun-bleached logs.

We sit as butterflies flit to find
flowers, blossoms, anything sweet.
Printed pages blur as sleep takes over,
and no one cares. No clock to punch,
no projects to complete.
I'm done, retired six years ago,
free as these birds and bees.
Next time I'll come with paints, and take home
plein air treasures, perhaps to sell or give to friends.

*Back Story: Retirement for me came in
summer 2008. Writing and painting have
filled my time since then. Yet Christine
easily persuades me to hop in the MX5
Miata convertible for a country drive, to
predictably stop at one of the beaches.*

A GOOD AGE TO BE SMART

Never sure just how to feel about this ageing process.
There was a time that I was ever young,
Ten years seemed not to change me much.
It's different now.

Each year presents to me another troubling challenge.
Some pain, some memory loss, some worry,
Can't dismiss realities of time.
I'm different now.

Of course I'm grateful for the years and all I have achieved,
But successes once considered vital,
Seem immaterial to me today.
It's different now.

I measure every day by something I took for granted.
Relationships mean more to me than I could have imagined,
Christine, my kids, grandkids and friends.
I'm different now.

LIFE IS CHANGING

Life is changing and I struggle to adjust to what I'm feeling.
Too much time to think about the low cards life is dealing.
I'm not ancient but I'm ageing, and I think of what will be,
Not a good approach to living, to reflect on what I see.

The world's economy is tanking and the globe is in recession.
Federal bailouts of big business trying to keep us from
Depression.
Haven't worried for a long time what might occur tomorrow.
Since my children became adults, haven't felt the need to
borrow.

I'm not working. I'm not earning, and the prices spiral higher.
Didn't care once what the cost was; now I'm a careful buyer.
Have a feeling that our savings will not be enough to make it,
And the feeling's getting stronger, seems no way for me to
shake it.

'Take no thought about tomorrow nor the clothes that you
shall wear,'
Is the counsel I've given others when I had so much to share.
'Don't be anxious but in all things with thanksgiving tell the
Lord,'
Believing that your next need will be one He can afford.

(Next Page)

I have no reason yet to panic though investments took a hit.
They say recovery's round the corner and will claw back bit
by bit.
Haven't got so long to wait until the market turns around.
Want to travel while our bodies are still reasonably sound.

Coffee mugs in hand we ponder, what our next move ought to
be.
Should I find work or end my life as an idle retiree?
It's a toss-up when we consider that the government will take,
Some of what they give us, when they don't give us a break.

*Back Story: Written in January 26, 2009. Markets crashed in 2008.
The latter lines are more germane today than a decade earlier.*

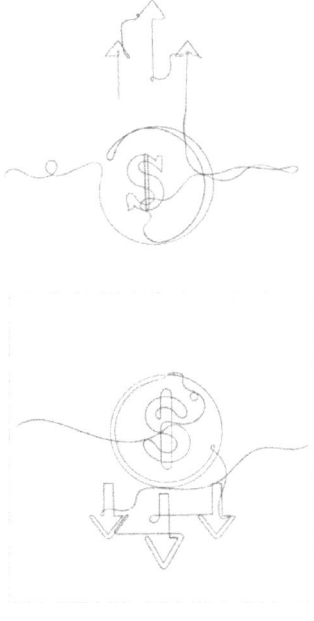

UP & AT IT

This body, this mind, awakened at night,
    recurrent morning restiveness
    when silence is my buddy, we agree.
Only the impassive hum
    of fridge and laptop impose upon
    these hours with black coffee, strong and hot,
    and pages I am reading,
    or words that I am crafting.

Familiar with 3 a.m. emails from me,
    my friends sometimes wonder loudly,
    why I am up at unearthly hours.
Somehow, I am quite at rest,
    and it's time for another cup.
I've put in two hours already,
    and I'm glad I am alive.
I think I'll go to the gym now.
After all it's 5.

GIVE ME A BREAK

Never mind sleepless in Seattle.
A little north of there,
someone else is wakeful at an early hour,
Me, and it's two a.m. in British Columbia.

I hit the sack at ten and slept with ease,
until nature called me to attention,
and waking, I found it was only eleven p.m.,
good reason to return to bed with covers pulled high
and try to sleep again,
for that was all it was, a mere attempt.

A neighbour was felling trees next door,
or breaking rocks,
or something that effectively disturbed me,
so, I played Farkle for a time,
then read some poetry by Al Purdy,
that led me to this moment,
when I record my sleepless battle.

Back Story: This was written in
December 2014. Ten years
later, I've turned the solitude of
early hours into my most
productive writing time.

UNTIL

Life never seemed as complicated,
Until I moved to this place.
Sold our private detached house,
And downsized to our small space.

Life never seemed as populated,
Until I came to this home.
From every unit daily
Countless dogs and people roam.

Life never seemed as regulated,
Until bylaws issued here.
Now a strata council makes
Misdemeanors very clear.

Life never seemed as insulated,
Until enclosed with people
But they're extremely private
Unlike folks beneath a steeple.

Life never seemed as abbreviated,
Until I came to this time
Retirement's closing chapters
Numerous years past my prime.

*Back Story: In 2012 Christine and I sold our large home and
downsized to a small-ish carriage home in a strata housing
complex. It required some adjustment... like the last 11 years.*

WHERE WE LIVE

This verse is prompted by a young woman's death
whom we honoured today, a neighbouring friend.
Didn't occur to us she'd breathe her last breath
and at age thirty-six, her young life would end.

So much heartache near our twelve hundred square feet.
Much more than seven years since we moved here it seems.
Then our quiet neighbours on our quiet street,
enhanced our pleasure in the home of our dreams.

Here, this complex of high-density living
Our private property becomes merely common,
when we hear disputes, threats, and no forgiving,
sirens of approaching medics and lawmen.

Two women we know have lost their health to booze.
A young girl suffered from an hourly seizure.
A boy would not wake due to drugs he would choose.
Such are events of my retirement leisure.

And yet we have found here so many good friends
Who if we had misfortune, they'd shed a tear
One must see this place through a positive lens
So to the extent we can help, we are here.

*Back Story: After a lifetime of service, we thought retirement meant
a pause. We downsized to a strata housing community. Close
neighbors share life stories. Responding to needs is our reflex.*

WHAT A DIFFERENCE A DAY MAKES

This morning these were my thoughts as I walked
Through the sunshine and shadow along my way.
Because yesterday I walked briskly with ease,
Whereas pain hit me with each step today.

'What a Difference a Day Makes,'
The title of an old popular song,
Told how twenty-four little hours
Remedied everything that was wrong.

Around the globe in villages, cities and towns
People find that one day is all that it takes
To turn one's good world upside down.
'What a difference a day makes.'

Instead of their wrong world being made right,
A collapse, a crash, a death alters lives.
A failure, a breakdown, a breakup shatters
Sons and daughters and husbands and wives.

Small wonder that a songwriter long ago penned
The words Dinah Washington sang so well.
When the dark side of life is pushed away
It's a story each one of us wishes to tell.

*Back Story: 'What a Diff'rence a Day Makes', a popular song
originally written in Spanish by María Grever. English lyrics written
by Stanley Adams and popularized by Dinah Washington in 1959,
for which Dinah won a Grammy award.*

WHAT IF? IF ONLY ... ISN'T THAT GOOD?

The shade grows darker, what if I won't see?
The sound fades further, what if I won't hear?
The hinges hurt, the digits ache, what if I won't bend?
The heart hurts, what if won't live?

I've seen it in my others, loved ones all, till then.
Admired them, respected, saw them tall, then small
As I grew manly, for my turn, to live and be and do.
And now it's almost done, this life, I feel, I know.

I write their story and my own, unfinished now,
With time I dream I still can do, so much, much more,
And better than before, with wisdom gained with age.

The younger come, so vibrant, eager, innocent.
If only they will listen, if only I will say
All that can help them, all I've learned along my way.

Patent is the cycle, sequenced through the ages.
Lives lived, stories told, learnings cited, wisdom posed.
Did I read, did I see, did I listen well enough?
Now, what if they won't see, what if they won't hear?
What if I must watch their mistakes and then shed a tear?

But what if I just show my love with every day I spend,
And see their triumph and success before my life can end,
Isn't that good? Isn't that best? Isn't that worth it all?
I see, I hear, I move with ease, I live.

UNDER PLASTIC

No safer place for him to be,
City bench, lying conspicuously concealed mid-morning,
Covered in ground sheets and plastic,
Corner of 200th and 64th with non-stop traffic
Twenty feet from his face, he is undisturbed,
Unconscious, better to sleep the hours away,
Than to live them hungry and destitute.

His bike leaning against his obscured form,
He'll know if someone tries to lift it.
Shopping cart full of belongings, his stuff.
No one else would care to keep.
No one who knew him knows him now.
No one asks how he feels. No one stops to check.
Lights turn green and he's forgotten.

Until he's up and someone sees him in the rain
Sitting near MacDonald's with plastic over his head,
And asks, "would you like something to eat?"
The answer is "yes," and minutes later
That someone reappears bag in hand,
Quarter pounder with cheese, and a coffee.

"Thank you, thank you … you're a good person."
And so is he, so was he back then
Before he got lost in life, lost from family, insecure.
He talks to himself now, loud enough that others hear,
He is his own best friend, and where will they be
Tomorrow.

THE WESTERN HEAVENS CRY

Rain gently wetting all that's green and dry
Celestial notice that the heavens cry,
Ending our slow summer days in the sun.
Anguishing at what humanity's done.

Drone-carried missiles exclusive of sound
Spray innocent blood on contested ground;
Guiltless targets rapt in their work and play.
Comes violent death on this routine day.

Inner-city violence, selfish greed,
Wanting and getting is distinct from need,
Culture bereft of security,
Few children survive to maturity.

Virulent diseases ravage the earth;
No one could dream how much water is worth;
Entire nations lack necessary food;
Disasters transpire as the heavens brood.

Absorbed in privilege we may ignore,
How helpless other humans are offshore.
We don't pause to think, content as we live,
But their brief lives measured by what we give.

Back Story: Sadly, since this was written a decade ago, and as I look at the world today, it appears little has changed.

MIRROR, MIRROR ON THE WALL

Mirror, mirror on the wall
Once you were my friend
I loved the way you made me look,
Whatever was the trend.

>Mirror, mirror on the wall
>No matter my style of hair
>Every time I looked at you,
>A handsome stud was there.

Mirror, mirror on the wall
I led a busy life,
And what you're showing me today
Cuts me like a knife.

>Mirror, mirror on the wall
>Why couldn't you be kinder?
>As I transformed from that to this
>I'd have liked a reminder.

Mirror, mirror off the wall
You've bullied me enough.
You can't disgrace me any more,
As I stand here in the buff.

>Mirror, mirror on the floor
>My nickname is the Slammer.
>Soon you'll have assorted parts.
>Meet my friend The Hammer.

2
LIFE AS I LIKE IT

WHILE WE CAN

A welcome Spring day yesterday,
the dreary sweep of callous winter done.
Our warm sun and the cloudless sky
summoned our top-down four-wheel transport
to the beach where seafood and a stroll awaited.
Hand in hand as it can be and should be
And as we like it.

*Back Story: We have owned 2 generations of MX5 Miatas,
1999,2007. At age 60 I wanted a motorcycle. Christine persuaded
me to have a sportscar. The best & safest idea, and fun for us both.*

A GOOD DAY FOR LIVING

As summer days go this one is good
with sunshine tonic for my mood,
and Pacific air to revive my drive,
I'm delighted to be alive.
Tranquil morning invites my time,
sometimes prose and sometimes rhyme,
composing words as spa tunes play faintly,
wordlessly through summer's day.

ALONE AND I LIKE IT

This is a day when the desire is gone.
Ideas come of things to do, of projects to begin,
But there is no will.
Indolence seems frivolous but it feels good.
I've been left alone, and I like it.
I savour the silence.
No intrusions allowed into this mute space.
I won't answer the phone if it rings.
I'm not checking emails or Facebook or Twitter called X.
Free to do anything, or something,
I choose to do nothing.
I can choose to snooze, to read, to reflect, or to take a sip.
Moments like this are hard to come by,
But these are mine, all mine, mine alone.

Back Story: This is applause to self-indulgent me-time days. We all need them occasionally. You know what I mean don't you? That's right. We aren't entirely indolent. When the day is done, we'll pick up our share of the load again. But for now, leave us alone.

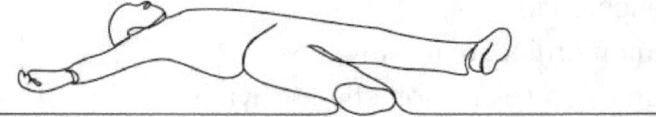

TREES ARE FOR CLIMBING

I was a boy when trees were tall,
and I could climb with ease.
High in the limbs though I was small,
At home in tops of trees.

My space did not require a friend,
Had no desire to share,
Or teach to climb or to descend,
Would only say "beware!"

Up there were stories of my mind,
A novelist was I.
I the hero, the dazzling kind,
With empires in the sky.

All stories end and so did mine,
Not wasted time at all,
A bold step to maturity,
When childhood trees were tall.

A HAIKU MEDLEY

Front Story: A Haiku form of poetry is known for its syllable count, 3 lines with 5,7,5. It's minimalist, disciplined writing. It derives from Japanese Hokku poetry. Each 3-liner intends to paint a vivid picture. They comment about the season or surroundings of the author. A haiku often has a kireji or 'cutting' word, an impact word. English writers adopted Haiku with some modifications.

Yesterday mountains
Bright with the sun's reflection
Brilliant for my eyes.

Morning dark becomes light
Time to walk in wintry cold
Still waiting for snow.

One loop round the pond
Resident ducks are at home
Undisturbed by me.

Silence like a cover
Gives me opportunity
For contemplation.

It's good and its bad
These thoughts, some pain, others ease
Outdoors, I'm dealing with life.

"I love you tomorrow"
The song sings to the future
I believe I will see it.

TOP OF THE MORNING

Sweetheart delivered my morning hug,
Familiar now, no youthful fainting.
Hot Coffee in my Tom Thompson mug,
With printed image of his painting.
A quiet start to an easy day
I leisurely gaze through misty blur
A distant pine tree with gentle sway
A black crow sits on its topmost spur.
From two hundred feet above the ground.
He surveys the realm of human homes.
Drew my attention without a sound,
Found his way into one of my poems.

THUNDER

I grew up with thunder, fascinated,
boyhood storms with claps and flashes,
warm summer squalls and autumn tempests,
charmed by the pelting cadence.
Saw the flare, then counted, one, two, three,
a jolt of cannon fire,
shaking glass, cracking trees.
Then silence in the rainy land
To which I moved years ago,
Where thunder is seldom heard
but for this morning.
At five o'clock, rush of rain outside
and unexpectedly the welcome sound
of thunder.

I OBSERVE HER

She wakes customarily with a smile.
Her early morning pattern begins an easy pace,
Turning the shades, as light fills space she prepares her
morning coffee.
She sits in one of two window seats savouring her brew and
thinking,
Private contemplations as well as those I will hear later.
Those quiet morning moments eventually lead to action and
to prayer.
Short time passes, now she sits with her journal as she has
done for years,
Filing anecdotes and disquiets, joys and prayers that I have
never seen.
I have respected her so much that in all these fifty-two years
together,
I have never peeked. I probably never will, even if she leaves
first.
I'm too afraid of what I'd find, perhaps ways I have
disappointed,
And yet I reason we've made treasured memories,
They must be in there too. Perhaps I'll never know.
Her Bible, companion to her journal, informs her as she reads,
Helps her to interpret and assess what's happening in her
world.
Confidently now she unfolds her day, chores and phone calls,
Grandchildren to pick up, friends to meet, shopping and
meals.
Her schedule rapidly fills and tests her managed health.
Limitless ideas and lavish energy have been her trademarks.
Ideas now must cope with more limited supplies.

*Back Story: Christine has lived so well, so honourably, devoted to
her LORD and her children and grandchildren and so many others
around her. She has done this quietly.*

IF ONLY THEY KNEW HER

With waspish waist and confident stride she moved
long legs under pleated skirts.
Cascading over her shoulders, brunette hair framing
the smile that made a whole room happy.
I wish my children could have seen her.
I wish they could have known her, then,
when she sang, a trained voice, young, still finding its way,
with promise of joy and triumph,
with fresh faith in God, strong and enough to carry
a wife, a mother and servant through adult years.

Grandchildren know her, only now
as she is to them, looks to them, lives for them.
Unaware of who she was and how life shaped her,
she is their Nana from their births,
their Grandma of the loving embrace,
absolute love and generous spirit,
They know enough. She makes them happy.

THE HIGH NOTES

If I could only sing the high notes
I would soar.
I would float a song to melt a mood,
Discordant with hard times;
I would lift a tune beyond the moon,
Where lovers lift their eyes;
I would glide a melody so long
That broken hearts would mend;
I would hum a bar so sweetly,
You'd wish it would not end.

33

ANOTHER YEAR OLDER

My daughter had a birthday,
A milestone you might say.
Last night we celebrated,
We ate and sang and toasted.
I celebrated her,
A special woman now.

I remember when Cari came,
Her sapphire eyes and soft snow hair.
Creative life of promise, devotion, music, joy,
Heart of love for family, children of her own,
A heart that survived an attack.
She's a precious woman now.

Viewed as rude to name her year,
Her age makes my seniority clear.
So I can't tell you how old she is,
But she's not 44 any more.
Cari's an exquisite person now.

*Back Story: This was written exactly ten years ago. Cari's going to
kill me now. She knows how much I love her. Maybe I'll get away
with this.*

OLD MAN 2

At sea by choice
Like Hemingway's Old Man
Yet so different.

He, fishing, enduring, surviving,
Me, cruising, enjoying, surfeiting.
Okay, slim similarity then,
Except love for the expanse
Of sapphire to the horizon
Far as I may gaze.
The sky, bright to the east
Soft gossamer clouds hinted distantly.

Navigated for me, I ride the Silhouette,
Without splashing spray in my face,
But rather, high aboard deck six
My balcony as large as the Old Man's vessel.

His hands raw from seizing the rope
To hold his giant fish.
My hands ache from osteo arthritis
For now I am an Old Man too.

Back Story: As a teen I read Ernest Hemmingway's 'Old Man and the Sea.' I felt so sorry for this aged fisherman who caught the largest fish ever seen in the area, only to have it shredded by hungry sharks before he reached shore. En route from Alexandria to Napoli, I wrote this while aboard a cruise ship in the Mediterranean Sea, a very different sea experience.

REMEMBERING RON

Once young men sharing a first name,
Ron he was, as was I, youthful and strong,
sharing faith, sharing laughter, sharing life.
Hours and days, our hopes and our dreams,
values in common and college ahead.

His '47 Plymouth coupe restored
in time for the road that led us both
into manhood, marriage, training and careers,
caring for people and God, a lifelong motivation.

In the years of our lives, we familied, achieved,
schooled further, travelled, each on our own,
disconnected by distance and different worlds,
seldom enjoying each other's coups and costs, and
then he was done in 2005 and I in 2008,
work set aside to retire, still provinces apart.

Now he is gone,
fulfilling the hope he promised to others
for decades with passion he spoke, God's truth.
I, in process still to meet him,
one day closer and then eons to share.

*Back Story: in memory of my boyhood friend, Ron Schindel, who
passed away on Sept 2, 2012 and whose family memorial service
was held at 1:00 PM September 6, 2012 in Linden, Alberta.*

WHAT DUCKS TEACH

Canvasback, Mallard, Merganser and Goldeneye
By nature requiring no comradeship bond
No navigation travel plan to certify,
Serenely cohabiting a city planned pond.

Like others, I make this my daily route.
Two legged and four-legged silent land-walkers
So laden with troubles that we want to shout,
Tramping in Salomon, New Balance and Dockers.

Envious of the placid waterfowl pace
No thoughts of relationships soured with time,
CBC, CNN, Fox News, have no place
When sculling in clear water rather than slime.

These ducks unlimited, free to fly or swim,
Inspire the offloading of bothersome thoughts
By land-huggers like me for whom life appears grim
When I can't see clearly to connect the dots.

Then light as a feather, having shed our concern,
We lift off like ducks, not a care in the air.
From that high pitch we can easily discern
A calm landing spot that we humans can share.

NO WORLD NEWS HERE

Soothing symphony of the ages
Rhythmic constancy, waves meeting shore
News free, I'm turning a novel's pages.
Removed from media, who needs more?

With a random glance I see otters
On a nearby raft they groom and dine
Diving for prey in icy waters,
Ocean seafood infused with brine.

It's what this whole week has been about,
Time to ponder, time away from cares,
Watching logs wash in and tides go out,
Place feels like ours even tho it's theirs.

These two people, big-hearted friends
What they have they hold with loose grip.
What each has acquired, each keenly lends,
Gifting us with this peace-giving trip.

*Back Story: A seaside cottage owned by
friends who have often opened it for
Christine and me to enjoy for a few days.
And we aren't the only beneficiaries of
their kindness.*

WHAT A GOOD MORNING

It's a morning of uncommon brilliance,
With clear skies at the eastern horizon,
Permitting the searing Sun to ascend,
Blasting vermilion in all directions,
Igniting undersides of stratus clouds
Reflecting red on placid seas below,
Where tug and barge plow near the distant shore,
While three otters frolic closer to me.
This tranquillity spins out silently.
Such a scene so far from my urban home,
Itself pleasant but rooms without a view,
And with thick traffic and construction noise.
Solitude should last longer than this week.
We won't be missed, maybe we won't go home.

Backstory: Enjoying a cottage week on Vancouver Island with seawater at the shoreline. Only four days remaining.

ZOOM, ZOOM March 2nd.

We cruised with the wind,
Luminous in the sun
And only March, an early spring
Room for two, an ideal number
After a lifetime filled with people
Top down, our sports car took us
To Porter's Bistro Coffee and Tea House.
Apple Strudel, Strawberry and Rhubarb,
And on to White Rock and Crescent Beaches.

SCRIBBLING MORNING THOUGHTS

Stringy cumulonimbus clouds fifty thousand feet aloft
motionless, with speeding altostratus billows beneath.
Swallows frolic effortlessly above the tallest cedar
while on the ground shrewd crows forage for edibles.
Seven o'clock sun has moved to warm my body,
and I enjoy the quiet of a people-less morning.
No one has moved outside, not even dog walkers,
but hummingbirds come to savor a drink between flights,
to other morning risers who relish visits from whirring wings.
I sip another long take of dark coffee, its aroma alien
to this air, fresh and new with the day.
Tree leaves lavish and blooms large with colour,
the month of May has not yet come to its end.
My mind is filled with the pleasure of life and sight,
the awe of enormity and distance, of infinity and perpetuity,
The acuity of small creatures in a hostile world,
the astonishment that humans have a home in space,
and gratitude we put seeds in the ground, and have an earth
for which we are responsible, and we get to see things grow.

LUNCH AT CRESCENT

I turn our sports car to the sea at Crescent Beach.
Scattered clouds can't hide the springtime sun.
Relaxed observers, we've come for lunch in our two-seater,
With sandwiches from Beast and Brine.

We're looking toward Vancouver, and the tide is out.
Curiously, not everyone notices or cares.
A sporty Honda pulls in beside us with two young people
who stay for fifteen minutes, each silently scrolling a
cellphone.

On our other side rap music beats and lyrics sound
as two young happy men keep a ball in the air,
their girlfriends soundly asleep in their car.
For them the breeze, the waves, the gulls have no effect.

Across the mud to the distant water, two dogs and a woman
walk.
She throws a ball the younger animal eagerly chases.
The older mate walks slowly, past his time for chasing,
Staying close to his master from whom he welcomes a pat.

Two trucks arrive and out climb eight people speaking
Filipino.
Soon two of them carry a boat motor the long walk to the
water.
Four others manhandle a Zodiac loaded with crab traps to the
motormen.
With motor attached two men in the boat sail to deep water.

With lunch over, we decide to walk on Blackie Spit.
Clamshells lie white and opened days ago by hungry birds.
Tidewater is coming in, still cold, yet one man wades knee deep.
Crescent Beach is pleasurable for everybody's reasons.

FORTY-SIX YEARS AND COUNTING

Under an arbor we once stood with roses
hanging overhead, her arm through mine, smiling
as cameras clicked to lock in time our poses,
on the day we said we do.

I bring morning coffee as she lies dreaming.
I turn to leave as she wakes with smiling eyes,
These forty-six years later she's still beaming,
looking forward to our day.

Under an arbor we stand in warm embrace,
so much that's different, so much that's the same.
I see without effort the love in her face.
Both consider ourselves blessed.

Back Story: I wrote this on August 12, 2013, to commemorate an anniversary, our forty-sixth. That was ten years ago. Last summer we remembered together, 56 years. This summer of 2024, it will be 57. We like it, and each other.

3
LIFE AS IT WAS

SOVEREIGNS OF THE STEEPLE

We climbed its rooftop,
Oblivious to risk.
Slate shingles slick as glass,
Pitched like a ski jump,
imposingly tall,
First Presbyterian Church.
No challenge to ten-year-olds,
Sure-footed in rubber soled
runners,
Gripping with fingers, bricks and ledges,
down spouts and edges,
Lithe and light bodies easily lifting our weight.
No one saw us, no one stopped us.
Timidity expelled from minds innocent of danger.
Nothing ventured, nothing gained until we conquered
the highest peak among all rooftops in the hood.

*Back Story: During the years from 1949-1956, I and my friends were
ages 7-13 in St. Catharines. Ontario. We were free spirits, fun-
loving, strong, sometimes stupid. On our bikes we felt like we
owned the city. Among our stories, this one too is true.*

FOUR BOYS OF SUMMER

Summer days and bikes and slingshots
Boyhood memories I choose to tell.
Beach and barefoot, hikes and slipknots
Retirement and grandboys partner well.

Four of us at unique stages,
Two boys, a pre-teen, and older gent
Three live lively while one ages.
They have forever while mine seems spent.

Our time together blesses both,
Me, inspired by their crisp touch on time,
For them, my tales and values nurture growth.
All four assisted to make the climb.

*Back Story: In 2013 my three grandsons were young, yet old
enough to walk with me through a forested park, through hollows
and up hills, and under branches, and stop for a sandwich in the
sunshine. I may be the only one of the four of us who remember
that.*

ANDREW WYETH TOUCHED MY TIME

I saw his work through a young man's eyes.
With untried hopes, my novice skills and promise showed.
I lived to dream where whims could lead,
Then Andrew's brushwork on published pages,
like holy scrolls I scrutinized.
His subjects evocatively rendered; unrivaled design.
Curtains in a breeze, a rust topped milk can,
weathered boots, all things of life where Wyeth lived.
With tempera and egg, he deftly laid them down,
celebrated pieces gaining national fame.
My obscurity and his renown.

I knew him where he walked, his habits and his loves.
Never met yet mentored truly to emulate his will
to paint the things I know and see and feel.
Four decades passed and I have come to paint again.
An older man with time I am,
and saddened by the news that Andrew's time is gone.
Yet with the time that was,
his emotion in a lifetime of treasured strokes,
an artist's legacy.

Back Story: I lived for my art as a youth,
believing that would be my life.
Andrew Wyeth's artistry was an inspiration to me. As God would
have it, I spent my life as a church pastor. In retirement I returned to
painting. On a January day in 2009 when Andrew passed away, I
reflected on his influence on me. It's a page in my life that I
remember with pleasure.

LOW NOTES MADE ME HIGH

From childhood into adolescence
I was a treble, a boy soprano.
The likes of Justin Bieber when he began.
My female sounding voice blessed to sing high C,
The defining note of a soprano voice.
I sang with ease and trained til I could touch an F,
One and a half tones above.
Then puberty insisted to interfere,
And the break occurred, a voice change,
Deepening my range by an octave,
So, by age seventeen I was baritone.

When younger my voice made young girls envious.
Now my baritone sound made them swoon.
So, at age twenty-four I sang love songs to her,
Followed by a question,
To which she answered "yes."
I can't complain when losing high meant gaining low,
Where vocal richness and fullness
Helped to win her heart.
And enhanced communication so important
To what I do – truth telling with conviction.
The Low notes have made me High.

Back Story: Some whimsical thoughts about true stuff. True that I won vocal contests as a boy soprano. True that my voice changed. True that I sang loves songs to Christine on our first date. True that I have taught the Bible which is truth itself. True she and I sing together.

HE KEPT HIS PROMISE TO HIS LOVE

Not coached like me to sermonize
my father spoke the finest words,
summoned from his life with her.

She lay unable now to answer, not needing to.
Intuitively he knew his time was short,
so aptly and prophetically he spoke his love.

His promise took our breaths away.

We, his loved ones in support,
ourselves now needing some assistance,
as he kissed her still cold face and said,
"Goodnight sweetheart, I'll see you soon."

Six months passed and he content
with children and grandchildren,
and he with life well lived and nothing more to keep him,
woke where his promise was fulfilled,
and where his Maker's promise led.

Back Story: On a November 2007 evening our large family gathered with our Dad after Mom died. Six months later Dad followed. He was 93 years old.

HALF-POINT MELTDOWN

Droning routines, annoyed with people, worn at the edges,
I recall time as unbearable in need of major change.
Should the change be disconnection from previous pledges?
A most plausible option tho admittedly strange,
I tried to ask but no one listened at all.

Unpredictably common this shared human occasion,
Half way through our fleeting lives, mortality comes knocking.
To be brave and hang in there demands robust persuasion,
Advice to hold tightly is morality talking,
Yet sometimes you don't care to listen at all.

I understand. I know that about which I'm speaking.
I myself suffered discontentment and confusion,
Sensitive tears flowed as my sad spirit was shrieking,
My heart and mind crippled by tortured disillusion.
At that blue time I couldn't listen at all.

The worst advice I received was from someone with money.
"Get a grip" was his obtuse counsel and his bottom line.
Healed and humorous now, at the time it wasn't funny,
"Take your time," from someone wiser; "and you will be fine,"
From one whose kind heart listened to all.

(next page)

Almost half a century since I found my way through.
Became aware of human despair where rest or change occurs.
Employed kindness to others from the distress by which I
grew,
Sharing patience, love, and peace - what a person prefers.
So, they were thankful that I had listened at all.

*Back Story: The poem revisits a crisis moment from four decades
ago when decisions were made around me that disappointed me
more than I anticipated. It taught me to be a survivor and it
equipped me to be compassionate to sufferers.*

VALENTINE'S DAY 2015

I'm not in denial, I know that I've changed,
All about me physically has been rearranged,
Yet my heart remains warm and I'm a romantic
Tho my style may be a touch tired and pedantic.
Why not give me a break, at least this time I tried.
It would have been nice if she broke down and cried.
Instead, though I sent her an e-link to my song,
I recorded online but it took me so long,
Working through so many electronic glitches,
She convulsed in laughter, and she was in stitches.
Between laughs she spoke, and she didn't talk a lot,
Just, "What would have been nice is a box of chocolate."
So there you have it, I was so proud of myself.
I'm putting that karaoke stuff on the shelf,
No longer serenading and playing the fool,
I've picked, 'Just Buy It, Don't Sing It,' as my new golden rule.

FIUMICINO, SEA TOWN

Overcast day – overnight rain, Friday,
Most pleasure crafts moored.
Marina life slow but for sailboats heading out to catch the
wind, crews of eight.

Trawlers dockside on Saturday,
A work day still, not on the waves but in port,
Repairing nets and ropes, scrubbing, maintaining,
A steady pace, some heavy but untiring, efficient
With animated Italiano, strong-voiced conversation
Through lips tightly clenching cigarettes, endlessly.

Ready for a new week here in Fiumicino,
Home of fisherman, out early each morning
Returning at 1800 hours to waiting locals and merchants
Eager for the day's catch,
Transferred to patrons in Rome and nearby ristorantes.
The fragrance of sea mingles with diesel and tobacco.

Presently it looks like a rain again, announced by sizzling
lightning,
Crashing clamor and rain storms like a dropping veil,
Moving shoreward, so sailboats turn and head for home.
Waiting, all of us, long enough and the sun appears once
more.

*Back Story: Christine and I have enjoyed numerous cruises on the
seas of the world. From our hotel in Fiumicino, we could walk and
watch a typical day in the Italian port.*

CHRISTINE AND ME AND OUR GRANDCHILDREN

What will they be, these fledgling treasures?
Once so helpless, not any more.
Each month changes in subtle measures
Make it difficult to ignore.
The truth that our lives are declining,
Their lives are reaching for their peak.
Proficiencies and skills refining
Each one unique while we're antique.
Might we survive until they marry,
Our grandkids with careers ahead?
Might we their tiny babies carry,
Before at last we go to bed?
We pass to them that when we rest,
We own a hope for life above.
Their own faith our preferred bequest
For our invested faith and love.

Back Story: These sentiments were expressed when our five grandchildren were young, and Christine and I were becoming accustomed to grandparenting. As I place this poem here now, our grandchildren are adults, four are at work and one completing high school.

UMBRELLAS UP, SMILES ON

I'm up, slept late, what's the time? Siri says eight,
Missed the horn from the five o'clock train.
Rained all night, raining now,
Seventy-two hours, a three-day rain.

I'm out for my walk, cool and wet as it is,
School children and escorts on their way.
"Morning," they say and smile,
Smiling back, I say, "Have a nice day."

Two male back-packed teens with their music playing,
Enter the park by the pond, talking.
Backpacks off at a bench,
Both smile at me as I keep walking.

I cross the street as a grade sixer passes,
Just like a grandpa is how I look.
Secure, she smiles at me,
As I pass her on this path I took.

A husband and wife whom I see ev-ry day,
She steps behind his lead as they pass.
We smile at each other,
They yield the sidewalk and walk in grass.

Dogwalkers come and go, they have to get out.
Each one nods with a hint of a smile.
I'm walking to lose weight,
Counting by steps and not by the mile.   (next page)

It's still raining now, my umbrella worked well.
Smiles seemed to bring out the sun today.
Yes, distanced and unmasked,
We're safe and we'll be back on Tuesday.

Backstory: It's wonderful to be able to see people smile. A common school day during the gloomy coronavirus pandemic is not so ordinary. Masks are mandatory in most public indoor spaces and optional outside our homes when walking and respecting one another's space. February 202. Poem Form is 11,9,6,9 syllable stanzas, with 2nd and 4th lines rhyming.

DAY SURGERY

I have had it done. Tho medical offices I abhor. For many months I've been very sore. No longer something I could ignore. I couldn't bear it anymore. I had bought pre-numbing from the store. That cost to me was 5 dollars times 4. The doc came in and shut the door. This doctor's job is an ugly chore. He told me to take off the clothes I wore. I left my shoes there on the floor. My doc and I have good rapport. Pain is something I deplore. I wanted a pain-free guarantor. He took his tools from a side drawer. Clamps and gauze and a razor. He bent down to explore. With his first needles I almost swore. Then he cut and cut and cut some more. Big time nasty uber galore. I wanted to clobber my doctor. Tho I was brave and didn't roar, from his office I quickly tore and in a few minutes, I was out the door. It's now the day after the day before. Still feel like I am saddle sore. Or been injured in a war. Dreaming of a distant shore, weary and sleepy to the core. ZZZZ ZZZZ ZZ snore.

Back Story: That's an appropriate term, since this prose poem remembers a hemorrhoid surgery, so perhaps you can smile at the whacky, even juvenile approach.

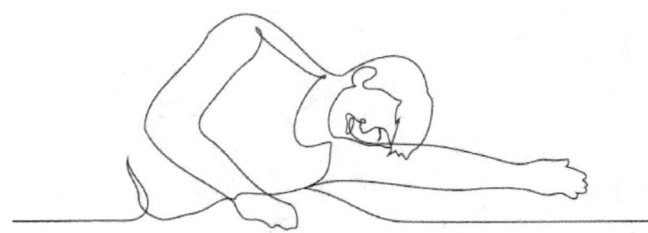

MOMMY'S HOUSE

From the moment she wakes,
she's preoccupied. Eagerly,
she readies herself to go.
Today is the day and tonight is the night,
she'll be sleeping at Mommy's house.

Pajamas, tooth brush, a child's cosmetics,
fresh undies and a change of clothes,
She remembers well and she packs her own bag.
Today is the day and tonight is the night,
she'll be sleeping at Mommy's house.

She cannot contain her excitement.
Her eyes wide, bright, and her breakfast down,
She waits, bag beside her, then her ride arrives,
because this is the day and tonight is the night,
she'll be sleeping at Mommy's house.

Captive princess, she's chauffeured,
Arriving to be encircled in a mother's love.
Quickly into her pajamas she changes,
Her own insurance that tonight is the night,
she'll be sleeping at Mommy's house.

A day filled with activities,
Fun things for a girl and her mom,
Baking cookies, watching videos, reading a story,
Normal things in an abnormal time,
And tonight, she's sleeping at Mommy's house.   (Next Page)

Back Story: This is true. An 11-year-old autistic child named Ayn climbed a fence and wandered from home. She was found in a neighbour's yard 3 hours later. She was safe. However, the Ministry of Children took the child into custody for three years. Yes, 3 years. This poem was written on a day when after that punishing separation, she was allowed to stay overnight at her mother's house. It took another year before she came home permanently. For 3 years I wrote regular blog posts advocating Ayn's parents appeal to recover their daughter.

TITANIC LOVE

Crippling. My private burden weighs a melancholy on me,
a daybreak desolation that may govern all I do,
unless trustingly I take respite in a promise someone gave me
whose existence is secured to me with paranormal glue.
Love so titanic, He relinquished all that mattered to him most,
whose approval means more to me, than makes any kind of
sense,
and before whom I grant freely, I have nothing of which to
boast,
yet who said there is forgiveness to a person who repents.

With that reminder I restart this twenty-four-hour day,
Now bursting with potential for an unexpected outcome.
Since my assets are empowered in a supernatural way
Everything that transpires will be thankfully welcome.

UNTIL THEY GO

Time crawls for me, ponderously slow
Since threats were made and worries grow
Since they came looking for the one
Who publicized what they had done.

They received notice, so must leave,
And their departure will relieve
Concerns of residents in this place,
That crime invaded our shared space.

Respectable renters are what they seem,
When really, they're a lawless team,
Opening their door to countless users,
Losing security, we all are losers.

Will they still seek revenge I wonder?
Will my proaction be a blunder?
Time will tell, two days to go,
Until month end when I will know,
I'm safe or not.

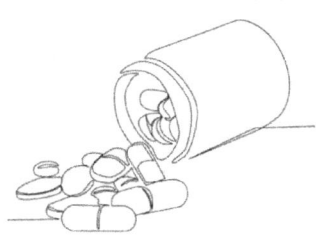

Back Story: Reflecting on intimidation that occurred for me from apartment residents in one unit who were illicitly selling drugs to daily customers to whom they gave access to our buildings, increasing unease and risk. And I, foolishly it seemed later, took photos of buyers. Drug dealers don't take kindly to that.

THE THIEF

Past flight and worry, he's been caught.
His ankles chained, unable to walk.
Waiting, condemned, his time soon comes.
He'll die today when come the drums.
Escorted swiftly to his cross,
Impaled in agony, all is lost.
He can't get down, he can't atone.
Never can he go back home.
Endures for hours and then hears Jesus
Speak the words with power to free us.
"*Remember me*," to Christ he cries,
Love's alive in Messiah's eyes.
True faith the Lord can recognize,
"*You will be with me in paradise*,"
The promise from the one beside.
Of him he'll say, "for me he died."
Death is no master, no need to fear it,
"*Into your hands I commit my spirit.*"

Back Story: A bad man, convicted felon found life as he died.

DEDICATION

'In memory of Murray,'
unthinkable words to write.
Often, I told Murray, "Mom always loved you best."
What was not to love about Murray? Blue eyes like mom's,
naturally curly hair, a beautiful boy. And then a beautiful man.
People responded with affection and attention,
to the man with a winsome smile and spontaneous humour.
Five years younger than me and solid friends in our teens.
Murray was friendly. God gave him friends.
He trustingly let God lead him in marriage and career.
Diane and Murray were a spiritual team.
It was more than good.
People found Christ because of Murray and Diane.
Not everything in life came easily.
Challenges and disappointments visited.
God managed the contests and always restored hope. Murray
faced his end of life, eternity occupied his mind, until the
moment hope converted to reality,
" like the morning sun, shining
ever brighter till the full light of day."

Back Story: Murray, my brother, five years younger than me, died in
November of 2023. This dedication was placed into my book, 'Like
The Morning Sun,' that was published Dec 1, 2023. Murray has
been teaching many of us how to deal with the end of life.

KNOWN HIM FOR HALF A CENTURY

Loves the ocean, water anywhere is a tonic,
for any reason, to fish, to swim, to kiteboard.
He loosens, releases and lets go, no longer focused
on the tortures, deep inside his anguished soul.

Surrounded by friends, a best friend to many,
he is loved because he's lovely,
yet he's lost one and that one was his world,
and his emptiness is a chasm he cannot fill.

A man of capacities and character, learning persistently,
relentlessly seeking to help others,
even when he cannot help himself.

He can't do enough to keep himself afloat.
This economy like an ocean eroding his shoreline.
Will there be a solid place where he can stand?

There is a rock, time-honored, a real friend
to whom he clings with manly strength.
He won't let go, he can't.
He esteems a legacy of faith, and champions it for others,
those who come behind him, like him will listen
to the voice of He who walks on water.

*Back Story: I have known men with broken lives and sought to help
them mend. Only the impact of loss in my own life needing crazy
glue to repair the rupture, has taught me the pain this man and these
men, endure.*

4

LIFE AS IT WILL BE

WHAT WONDROUS LOVE

His hands are language calling from them,
Blended sounds he's coached to brilliance.
Their faces are exhibits of their elevated praise.

Their lives like soft clay for the shaping,
Our own lives fired to terra cotta.
Together we extol the Lord whose name their voices raise.

We are the ones who sit now to listen.
We are the ones who have travelled so long.
We are much nearer,
To the theme of their Sanctus
We soon will unite with the heavenly throng.

Back Story: Composed after hearing a musical liturgy featuring hymns and Schubert's Wind Mass and Elgar's 'Nimrod' from Enigma Variations presented by Trinity WU's Chamber Singers and Concert Band under direction of Joel Tranquilla.

BEFORE WINTER COMES

A boy soprano I could sing,
Unknown to me, this was my Spring.
When my fam-ly was all and I was young
And my whole life was a song unsung.
My childhood was easy, bright and new,
And boyhood concerns were extreme-ly few.
Content with little I was happy then,
Not knowing I would not feel this again.

To work I was a newcomer,
Did not think this was my Summer.
I graduated and I dated her,
Then marriage and children a seeming blur,
A home of our own and stability
Made fam-ly life a tranquillity.
A fulfilling career sped by so fast,
Before I knew it, four decades had passed.

Told myself I'd not hit bottom,
This was a blast, this was Autumn.
As coloured leaves fell and cooler winds blew,
Formal work wound down and leisure grew,
My focus was canvas, brushes and paint,
Even an artist can live like a saint.

(NEXT PAGE)

My remaining thin hair turned white with age,

Sales of paintings replaced regular wage.
Poem done, on goes the printer.
Must be ready, here comes Winter.

Must finish my books, my fam-ly's history,
What follows next is still a mystery.
My entire life long I have lived in trust,
That God will be near when my shell is dust.
Be patient with me as my mem-ry fades.
Know I loved you when death pulls down the shades.

Back Story: Spent my life as a shepherd of people. I wrote this poem at age 77, reflecting comfortably on the past, my past, and this place in time to which the years delivered me. I published my Family history book in December 2023, entitled, 'LIKE THE MORNING SUN.'

DREAMING FORWARD, WISHING BACK

"Who'd want to be fifty," they asked,
when I told them that's what I wanted,
and I was fifteen.
Had enough of teen years,
convinced they would not improve.
Why not skip the discomfort, I thought.
At fifty success and security were assured.

Yet now I'm thirty more than fifty.
I'm thinking inversely and fifteen wasn't bad.
I could eat what I wanted. Didn't put on weight.
Had hair I could style. Could run forever,
Could sleep through the night.
Could sleep in and nothing hurt.
I want to be fifteen again.

But I remember why fifteen sucked.
I was still in my folks' house. Couldn't drive the car yet.
Was attracted to girls but self-conscious.
Had stupid school for the conceivable future,
and then finding work and grinding work,
nd family and mortgage and stress,
And wishing for fifty plus and retirement.

(Next Page)

So I'm thinking it's okay where I am.

I lived a good life with a good wife,
who gave me two loving and talented children,
who gave me five adorable grandkids,
and I'm settled, no dreaming forward,
no wishing back.
It is what it is and I'm fine.

*Back Story: When I was fifteen, two of my aunts asked me what I
wanted to be, and I told them I wanted to be 50 years old. They
were perplexed and told me how much of life I would miss if my
wish could be granted.*

UNNATURAL FOR ME

Surf spilling forward in sequential waves,
And softly pitching thinning to the shore.
I, nearby musing on my waning life,
Each wave reminds me of a fleeting year.
One wave, one year, transient and then gone,
Yet the sea does not run out of waves.
I'd gladly give up my remaining years,
To certify my family would own joy.

Cloudless type of day when an eagle flies,
Lifts off the tallest tree to drift on air,
I dream I leave my highest point of life,
When nothing's left for me up there but glide
On currents warm and welcoming to me
Supremely high away from people's pain,
Gone from their cherished lives that gave me delight.
I can't bear what I can no longer change.

MY PAST ENDED LAST NIGHT

A long past upon which to cast nostalgic glances,
Despite incalculable benedictions,
Replete with wasted prospects, well-timed chances,
Squandered by imprudence, recklessness.
Shall grief consume my hours,
A choice to make as new days dawn.
Will I take hope or will I be
Harassed by faults and life that's gone?

With pardon, freedom comes for judicious decision.
I opt for the freeway of limitless joy,
A banquet of years exceeding my vision,
Can I be such a fortunate boy?
I refuse to look back.
Convinced my past ended last night,
I focus on a future track,
With outcomes astoundingly bright.

*Back Story: The title and the gist of the poem point to a philosophy,
a way of looking at life after a good portion of it has been lived. In
the sense that I am keen about the future and will not dwell on what
has preceded, the past ends with nightfall and sleep.*

ONE DAY I WILL SEE

Events I will remember,
For the few years left to me
Like when the clouds consumed me
And the sun declined to shine.
I thought my life was textbook,
All my relationships were seamless.
Thought nothing could disturb me,
That a life of bliss was mine.

I was a naïve young man.
The first time that it happened,
It took only four of them
To cause me to lose my job.
I thought I dealt with it calmly,
Moving on to a job much better,
Intermittently looked back,
Resolute not to sob.

That disappointment ended,
I enjoyed years of success.
Then suddenly I was terrified.
I discerned I could not cope,
Grieving with frayed emotions
Discouragement took me over.
No way I could carry on,
I found I had no hope.

I learned that life has potholes,

Over which I have no controls.
I have to trust in someone
Very much bigger than me.
I take nothing for granted,
Believing my life is guided
By the God who truly loves me
And whom one day I will see.

New chapters can be good ones.
Another one came along.
By then I was a middle-aged man,
I was strong and good to go.
Then, like a repeat it happened,
Several people set their plan.
They altered my tomorrow.
For me, a tragic blow.

Resilience has its benefits.
Mine, the privilege of a lifetime.
I was competent for it,
And I finished very well.
Only now in retirement
Something else unforeseen,
Has drained my reservoir of joy
Near to the final bell.

NEXT PAGE

I learned that life has potholes,
Over which I have no control.

I have to trust in someone
Very much bigger than me.
I take nothing for granted,
Believing my life is guided
By the God who truly loves me
And whom one day I will see.

Back Story: When you lose someone from your family, the entire clan suffers the loss for the rest of our lives. I love her and will miss her until I leave life.

MY WORLD IS BECOMING SOUNDLESS

In the silence of this Sunday morning
I hear the hummingbird's wings.
I notice that I can hear them.
I notice because I know a time is coming,
A time I fear when birds will come without a sound.
Without aids I can't hear them now.
Sometimes my sweetheart sits at her piano
And as she plays she sings.
I cannot bare the thought of her mouthing silent words.
I hear the repeated blasts of the Langley trains, quite shrill,
And I think at some time soon I won't know when they pass.
In no way can I prepare for this,
Other than with thanks now for hummingbird wings.

WHAT IF BLINDNESS

Christine, this morning as you spoke with a friend,
I stood on the street across from the square,
looking at distant condos, then close up buildings and people,
and street light poles and I thought to myself,
what if I was, or I am, looking at all of this for the last time.
It wasn't upsetting … it was pragmatic ... healthy …
It was an alluring experience, a blissful awareness,
I didn't want it to end; this consideration …
A last glimpse of ordinary and dated buildings on a late
October day.
So beautiful, and the finishing sight was enough for me.
I had peace. I've seen so much. Been grateful.
Looking forward.

*Back Story: Increasing eyesight difficulties over the past three years,
moved me to be realistic about the possibility of living without
vision. I have been very concerned. Medical professionals are
helping me. I will see what 2024 brings.*

A FRESH GLIMPSE

A new way of looking at life;
I say 'new' since it's unfamiliar
in this world of 'me' and 'mine,'
and I'm blemished by self-obsession.
The unveiling of this new way coincides
with my 80th birthday and a placid Pacific repose,
a coastal holiday, a retreat from thoughtlessness,
that has me thinking.

With the incoming tide, a new thought washes on me.
Four decades have come and gone since I came.
God gave me a body in which to live life.
Was His to give, His to take, His to change and to remake.
I used it, lived in it, as well as I could,
ever grateful to be reliably strong.

Now as weakness displays, my tendency is
to claim it's 'my' body as if it's a shame
to grow old and infirm, how dare my body be weak,
forgetting, life beyond life is what I seek.

And He is the One who decides it is time.
He who gave body and life, gave His word,
that by faith I would forever be with the LORD.

MY LONG GRIEF

The loss of one, the loss of a son,
The loss of a wife, the loss of a life,
The loss of a lover,
Slow to recover,
Becomes a long grief.

The hurt of absence,
The pain of empty,
The sound of silence,
There is no relief.

Don't cliché me to death,
Don't tell me 'don't cry,'
Don't say get a grip,
When I cry out 'Why?'
Mine is a long grief.

One day will pass and then another,
In some deficit way,
I will recover,
But I won't be the same.
My long grief laid its claim.

I'll smile again and help others grin,
Hiding the anguish I carry within.
I'll live longer and I'll live without,
But I'll always miss the one life was about.
'twill be a long grief.

(Next Page)

Back Story: My long grief is the testimony of many heartbroken

people I know, whose spouses have either died or left the marriage.
The daily grief from loss by death is heavy. The burden of
abandonment by a partner is unparalleled. Some recovery of
happiness is possible yet always there is the unrelenting memory of
love lost.

LOOKING FORWARD AT YEAR'S END

At precisely the stroke of twelve last night,
my birth year came to a progressive end,
seven decades furnished to me to tend.
I reflect on them with grateful delight.
I crowded this gift of years with child's
play, aspiring art and a loving wife.
Came children, studies, work, a selfless life
lived in service to others and God smiled.
Sounds immodest perhaps; I speak of call
from God to whom I've been obedient.
No option when seeing the greater gift
of Jesus who by dying gave it all.
Here I am January 1, conscious I've been given
years to invest and then divine uplift.

Back Story: These were my convictions and commitment as my 70th
year of life closed off on December 31, 2012. Eleven more years
have been added to my count. I am grateful.

A LONG YESTERDAY

A long yesterday are my years.
I'm frequently going back. I'm in a groove
reopening memories, revisiting friendships, re-entering scenes,
rethinking decisions, reflecting with satisfaction
on my lifetime spent suitably, but not done.
Yet going forward is a bullet train.
Only a few stops remain en route,
and I, with so many dreams to fulfill, maybe,
or maybe not before times up.
Here that is, and then, my faith's assurance, eternity.
I think of it, my life a vapour in contrast with forever
and whatever that can mean in company with the One
who birthed my being to reflect Him.
Have I done that well, I wonder?
I still have time, today, just now.
A long yesterday were my years.
Alive with Christ is my now and my future.

THEN BIRTHDAYS WON'T MATTER

Only weeks away from my birthday,
Approaching the end of my days.
Cheered by so much that has happened,
Disheartened in some other ways.

Three score and ten was the promise
I've exceeded that with nine more.
Yet perhaps there will be more time,
So I will count one score times four.

Wondering how I will finish,
When at last all my days are done.
Not anxious about the outcomes
My primary conflict's been won.

I've studied much that's been written.
I'm firm concerning the details,
To enter time that's unmeasured,
Where eternal living prevails.

Yes of course I'm a man of faith,
I trust in a transcendent God,
For the future that he has promised.
In his time I'll hear him applaud.

Not because I've been a good man,
Or that I deserve to belong
Only because he has loved me,
And he's been waiting this long.

(Next Page)

Back Story: Two years have passed since I wrote this. I was a boy when I heard a cowboy sing about heaven. He sang, "I've got so many million years I just can't count them." Later, I read Max Lucado's 'The Applause of Heaven,' in which he explored the Beatitudes, and Jesus' description of the coming sacred delights and enduring joy.

METAPHORS FOR MY AGEING THOUGHTS

Surf spilling forward in sequential waves
And softly pitching, thinning to the shore
I, nearby musing on my waning life,
Each wave reminds me of a fleeting year.
One wave, one year, transient and then gone,
Yet the sea does not run out of waves.
I'd gladly give up my remaining years,
To certify my family would own joy.
The joy that only comes by faith.

Cloudless type of day when an eagle flies,
Lifts off the tallest tree to drift on air.
I dream I leave the highest point of life,
When nothing's left for me up there but glide
On currents warm and welcoming to me,
Supremely high away from people's pain.
Gone from their cherished lives that gave delight,
I can't bear what I can no longer change.
"God, help them to choose joy by faith."

MAKING CHOICES

Life is about making choices.
I choose you still.
I chose you when I was young,
couldn't see past tomorrow.
You too had a choice to make.
Looking forward you chose me.
We talked about investing trust,
confidently chose to trust each other,
we pledged it for a lifetime.
Such an audacious prospect.
Since life's about choices, there were times,
you might have changed your mind.
Planet life offers many options,
I could have tripped on some,
but we both embraced our ageless choices,
so trust and promise won.

I now see many yesterdays,
today is where I live, and you are here.
If there will be no tomorrow,
today and yesterdays were enough,
because you chose me.

MY DEAR CHRISTINE, A MOTHER, MY WIFE

An astral voice with promise she
imagined a marquee to herald fame,
her name famous, yet
the primacy of faith and call to service, governed
choices, one of which was me.
>   This long legged beauty strode with
>   chestnut tresses, pleated skirts swaying,
>   into my heart until she walked an aisle
>   in white one August day, beginning
>   a life, a marriage, a motherhood.

To spaces, places far from home she
made a home, she was at home.
Charming adaptation to roles thrust hard
upon her, pastor's wife and mother,
her gifts seemingly unobserved.
>   Yet she coached others, not least of whom,
>   Her children, her love tattooed
>   forever on their hearts, they love
>   their children as she did them, and
>   countless others whose lives touched hers.

She could have been, she might have been, those
thoughts sometimes recur, then pale
before the faces of five sweet people, small, now
Growing, gone too soon, she'll be
remembered for all the memories she birthed.

*Back Story: This poem was written in 2014. Ten years later, our
grandchildren are no longer small. All have grown into gifted adults.
Through all the years, their Nana/Grandma has made a home in
each of their hearts. To her own children, she is the very best friend.*

GOD KNOWS EVERYTHING

God's knowledge is intuitive.
It's inherent to who He is.

God never has to read,
And He never has to learn,
Yet He knows all that is possible to know.
Everything that has ever been known,
Everything that can be known,
And all that will yet be known,
He knows.
His knowledge never changes,
And His knowledge never grows.
Perfect knowledge is inherent to the Lord.

God's knowledge is unlimited and comprehensive.
Omniscience is natural to God.
Nothing can be concealed.
He sees the sparrow when it falls,
And He knows the number of hairs upon your head.

Then why should you be afraid about the future?
As the bearer of His image
You are of infinitely more worth
Than all the pretty creatures He designed.
God has a vested interest,
And He has a perfect plan
Because He loved you before the world began.

WALKING EACH OTHER HOME

Christine and I have stepped off eight plus decades of time
while we have inhabited earth.
Our cadence was distinct and independent through our first
two decades of life and then we met.
Immediately we found a rhythm, a shared stride while dating
at college.
That uniform gait breezed us effortlessly past other sidewalkers
to graduation and marriage.

In unison we strode our way through unfamiliar terrain
illuminated by faith in One who advises our steps.
Came work. Came babies. Came Joys. Came hardships.
Mutual trust was fundamental to our ongoing unified pace.
Not easy for her to walk with a flawed partner
for whom perfection was imperative.

Not easy for me to recognize the defects in my own march.
I didn't see. Not then. I didn't see that she walked to my beat.
Always. I didn't see. She was entitled to tramp her own trail.
So gifted she was that her own walk could have taken her
farther, a trail not separate from, but conjoint with mine.
Thanks to her we trekked together. I didn't see. I didn't think.

She was patient. I didn't see and my culture didn't teach me.
Exceedingly patient, she. Wonderful she.
Along our dual journey it was I who received an honour here,
a recognition there. And she was always glad for me.
Yet she should have been applauded. She deserves such
celebration still.
Wondrous person, she, and I have sensed for a long time,

that though we walk together, it is she who sets the pace.
Challenges appear as time goes on and while our pace slows
down,
we each are content in knowing that we are walking each
other home.

*Back Story: I wrote this in 2019 and feel the strength and comfort of
the last two lines more profoundly today as this collection of poems
comes to print.*

ABOUT THE AUTHOR

Ron lives in beautiful British Columbia, Canada, together with his wife Christine, and very close to his children and five adult grandchildren. He drives an MX5 soft-top to saltwater shores at Crescent and White Rock Beaches as often as possible. He is an artist who paints portraits, and mountain, ocean, and vineyard scenery. He spent a lifetime working with words. He has been a spiritual shepherd and pastor to people in several congregations. Along the way he earned master's and doctoral degrees related to his altruistic service. He is a storyteller and perhaps some aspect of this poem collection has stirred you to consider deeply, how God is active in your own life, or how much more you want to experience Him.

Ron is the author of:
Crandall's Door, a novel for Young Adults aged 11 plus;
God in the Open, Colossians, devotional commentary;
The Eleven, My Interviews with the Apostles;
Why? Ecclesiastes: The Riddle of the Human Experience;
Like The Morning Sun, A Personal and Family Spiritual Portrait

Author Website: www.ronunruh.com
Artist Website: http://ronunruhgallery.webs.com